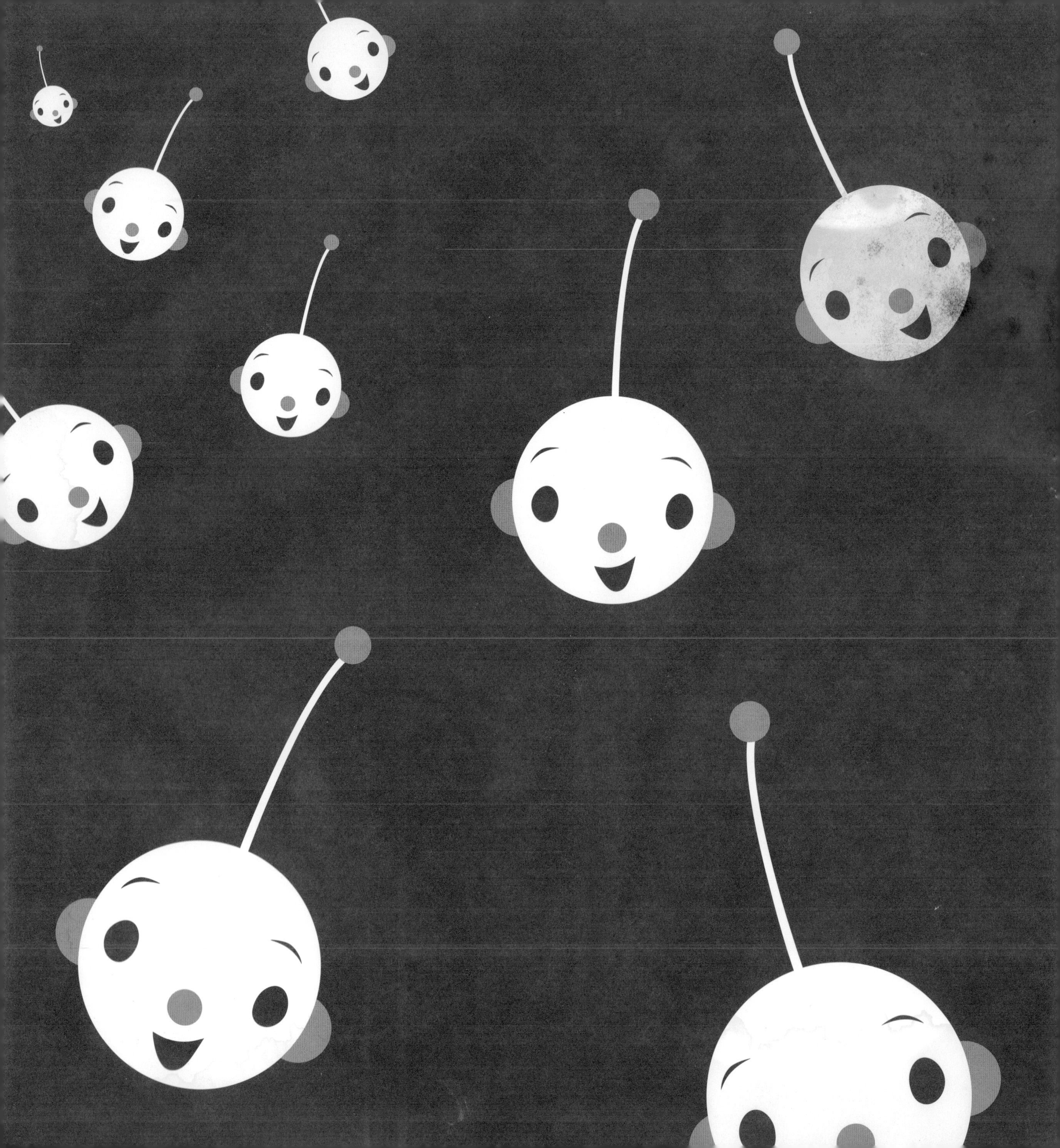

big time Olie
by William Joyce
LAURA GERINGER BOOKS
An Imprint of HarperCollinsPublishers

Rolie Polie Olie was sizing up
quite nicely.
In fact he grew a little bigger every day.
He even sang a song about it.

"I'm a little bit bigger,
Not a little bit smaller.
I'm a little bit taller—
I'm growing Rolie up!"

But when Mom and Dad took a trip to Mount Big Ball, they said Olie was too little to go—

which Olie thought was big-time unfair!

Then Pappy said he was too big
to jump on his bed
while eating ice cream.
So Olie shouted in his biggest voice,

"I'M NOT
THE RIGHT
SIZE FOR
ANYTHING!"

He was so unhappy.

He got a big and really bad idea.

He would use the shrink-and-grow-a-lator!

He twirled the dial.

He pulled the lever.

He pushed the button—

the wrong button.

He was in a little bit of trouble.

Zowie thought he was a dolly.

But Spot became
a Rolie rescue doggy!

Then Olie pushed the bigger button reeeeally hard.

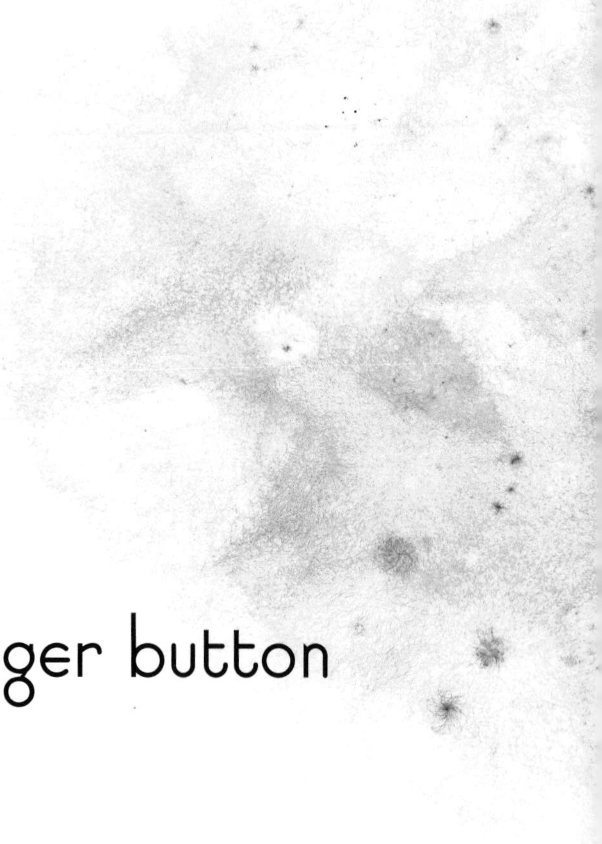

"Now that I'm grown up," he said,
"I'll do just what I want."

So he jumped . . .

. . . all the way into outer space,
where he got a scoop of ice cream
from the ice cream planet.

Then he bonked
his head on
the moon,

burned his bottom
on the sun,

and landed with a big
KABOOM!

He began to sing in his tiniest voice,

"I'm stuck on top of Mount Big Ball.
I'm lost and lonely and so tall.
I wish I could be back small.
I feel a little sad."

A big tear rolled down his Rolie cheek when he felt a tickle on his giant Polie tummy.

Then he smiled his biggest smile,
and with a push of one small button . . .

. . . he went back to being just plain Olie!

The trip home was long,
the Band-Aids were large,
and tiny tears were all wiped away.
Olie was so relieved to be home,
he sang a song about it.

"I was a sorry, sad Olie.
I've been a mad and bad Polie.
I won't be in such a hurry
to grow all Rolie up!"

Then he gave everybody
a big hug and big kiss,
and he went to sleep
in his bed that was just big enough . . .

. . . for now.

For
Big Time
Rich
—WJ

Special thanks to
the usual suspects:
Pam Lehn, Susie Grondin, Jordan Thistlewood, Paul Cieniuch, Gavin Boyle, Ian MacLeod, Brian Harris, Daniel Abramovich, Dave Simmons, Kelly Brennan, Don Kim, Sara Newman, Lisa Kelly, Alicia Mikles, Neil Swaab, Dorothy Pietrewicz, Ruiko Tokunaga, Tamar Brazis, Maria Lake, Emily Clark, Trish Farnsworth, Katie Dunkleman, Laura Geringer

THE ROLIE POLIE OLIE
ANIMATED TELEVISION SERIES IS PRODUCED BY
NELVANA LIMITED AND SPARKLING®

Big Time Olie

Printed in U.S.A. www.harpercollins.com
Library of Congress Cataloging-in-Publication Data
Joyce, William.
Big time Olie / by William Joyce.— 1st ed.
p. cm.— (Rolie Polie Olie)
Summary: Frustrated when his parents tell him he is too little for some things and too big for others, Olie decides to use the shrink-and-grow-a-lator.
ISBN 0-06-008810-9 — ISBN 0-06-008811-7 (lib. bdg.)
[1. Growth—Fiction. 2. Size—Fiction.] I. Title. II. Series.
PZ7.J857 Bi 2002 2002001270
[E]—dc21 CIP
AC
Typography by Alicia Mikles
1 2 3 4 5 6 7 8 9 10
❖
First Edition